F. E. Ware

Brown Bessie

F. E. Ware

Brown Bessie

ISBN/EAN: 9783337343231

Printed in Europe, USA, Canada, Australia, Japan

Cover: Foto ©Andreas Hilbeck / pixelio.de

More available books at **www.hansebooks.com**

Λ

Drama in Four Acts.

By F. E. WARE.

— —

NEW YORK:
JOHN F. TROW & SON,
PRINTERS AND BOOKBINDERS,
209 EAST TWELFTH STREET.
1874.

BROWN BESSIE.

A Drama in Four Acts.

PERSONS REPRESENTED.

OSCAR ALMA.—Artist and lover of Mercy Wilde.
BARATOLI.—Conductor of opera.
THOMAS THORRINGTON.—English gentleman, aged seventy.
SIR WILLIAM AYELTON.—English gentleman, aged fifty.
LEDYARD THORRINGTON.—Nephew and heir to Thomas.
JACK HINTON,—Companion to Ledyard.
DEACON WILDE.—Supposed father to Mercy—farmer.
JOHN DIKEMAN,—Farmer, father to Brown Bessie.
WILL LITTLEFIELD, } Young men of the village.
MARK KENDRICK, {
SIME LETHRIDGE.—Boston rough—Captain of Knights of the Red Crescent.
MAXWELL.—Barkeeper,)
DENVILLE LOWBURY.—Knights of the Order of the Red Crescent.
RAB WETHERBE,)
BROWN BESSIE.—A child of great vocal powers.
MERCY WILDE.—Village beauty.
MADAM BARATOLI.—Mother of the conductor.
MADAM ELVA.—Jealous Prima Donna.
PAULINE.—Niece of Baratoli.
RACHEL SNOW.—Country gossip.
MR. JOHN STILWELL.—English gent.
MRS. ELIZA STILWELL.—Wife of the above.
OLD MEN, VILLAGERS, &c.

COSTUMES.

OSCAR ALMA.—(3) Hunting suit of green; straw hat. 2d. Gentleman's suit of black. 3d. Emb'd blue cloak, trunks, and white vest.
SEIGNIOR BARATOLI.—(3) Dressing gown and slippers. 2d. Suit, emb'd green cloak, white vest, and trunks. 3d. Gentleman's suit of black.
THOMAS THORRINGTON.—(1) Gentleman's travelling suit.
LEDYARD THORRINGTON.—(2) Gent's travelling suit. 2d. Suit of black.
SIR WM. AYELTON.—(3) Gent's travelling suit. 2d. Suit of black. 3d. Emb'd crimson cloak, trunks, and white vest.
JACK HINTON.—(2) 1st. Travelling suit of brown. 2d. Suit in black.
DEACON WILDE.—(2) 1st. Farmer's suit of blue; broad, white collar and straw hat. 2d. Suit in black.
JOHN DIKEMAN.—1. Farmer's suit of blue.
WILL LITTLEFIELD.—1. Farmer's suit of blue.
MARK KENDRICK.—1. Farmer's suit of blue.
SIME LETHRIDGE.—1. Gentleman's suit of black. Regalia of the Knights of the Red Crescent, a scarlet scarf thrown across the left shoulder fastened with a silver crescent on the shoulder; a silver star on left breast.
MAXWELL.—1. Farmer's suit, scarlet scarf and crescent.
DENVILLE LOWBURY.—1. Farmer's suit, scarlet scarf and crescent.
RAB WETHERBE.—1 Farmer's suit, scarlet scarf and crescent.
MR. JOHN STILWELL.—(2) 1st. Gent's suit of black. 2d. Page's suit of blue.
BROWN BESSIE.—(4) Country dress of faded calico, hat and shawl. 2d. Dress of crimson emb'd in gold. 3d. Travelling suit in black, straw bonnet, and shawl. 4th. White satin or silk spangled with silver.
MERCY WILDE.—1st. White dress and pink ribbons. 2d. Travelling suit. 3d. Pink dress emb'd in silver. 4th. Rich white silk, diamond ornaments.
MADAM BARATOLI.—Black velvet, studded with silver point-lace. 2d. Suit travelling dress in black, bonnet and shawl.
MADAM ELVA.—1st. Suit blue silk, plain. 2d. Suit orange silk, emb'd in silver.
PAULINE.—1st. Suit purple silk, plain. 2d. Scarlet satin or silk, emb'd in gold.
RACHEL SNOW.—1st. Gingham dress, white apron and cap.
MRS. WILDE.—Plain black dress, white apron and cap.
MRS. STILWELL.—1st. Suit morning robe in pink. 2d. Black lace, starred with silver.
PROPERTIES.—Apples—a pack of cards—a turkey—2 bottles of brandy—2 pistols—2 lanterns—a bracelet—books—a scaffold with rope—a pocket Bible—dinner-horn—cradle—mug of cider—glasses—dusting-brush—rope—packing boxes—pictures—easel—2 jewel cases—jewels, etc.

Entered according to Act of Congress, in the year 1874, by
L. D. SHEARS,
In the Office of the Librarian of Congress, at Washington.

BROWN BESSIE.

ACT I.

Scene I.—A Forest in Massachusetts.

Enters Brown Bessie, with bonnet in hand.

Bessie. Isn't it delightful, tho', to run off by one's self in the cool, quiet wood—and not a soul near to scold or find fault. Oh, if I had only been Eve, though, with all this wide world to myself, I reckon when Mr. Adam came around to pop the question he'd have got the mitten—that he would. [*Looks up in the trees.*] How happy the dear birds are, singing so merrily. I can sing too, and they all like to hear me. [*Sings.*

Enter Alma unperceived, listens.

Alma. Hilloa! my little songster, who in the name of all that is wonderful are you?

Bessie. [*Looking frightened.*] Oh, I'm only Brown Bessie; that's all.

Alma. [*Taking her hand.*] And that's considerable, according to my way of thinking. But who taught you to sing?

Bessie. The blue birds and the robins up yonder; they like to hear me.

Alma. So do I; and so will all the world if you will but give them the opportunity. Oh, if Seignior Baratoli had such a voice to cultivate, he would astonish the world.

Bessie. And who is this Baratoli?

Alma. The world-renowned tenor! Have you never heard of him, my little girl?

Bessie. Never, sir! I hear nothing but cross words and threats, and taunts of my own ugliness, from morning till night; except when I run away into the wood, as I have done to-day. Then when I get here in the cool refreshing shade and hear the soft music of the stream and the sweet songs of the birds as they warble in concert for me, I forget my troubles for an hour and warble with them. Oh dear! I wish I could always live right here in the wild wood, no more dishes to wash, no scrubbing, no housework, but rest and song the whole day long.

Alma. [*Aside.*] Here is a treasure for some one. I've half a mind to take her myself; but alas! what can a poor penniless artist do towards maintaining and educating a little wildling like this?

To Bessie. I say, little songstress, if you will coax your friends to take you to New York, and put you under the instruction of Seignior Baratoli, you will soon find yourself famous.

Bessie. Oh, that would be delightful. But then— papa will never let me go; and Sally—she beats me if I open my mouth.

Alma. And who the deuce is Sally?

Bessie. Oh, she's my handsome sister.

Alma. I'd like to catch her misusing you, my little bird-charmer; come! sit down, and let me make a sketch of you. [*Draws a book and pencil from his pocket.*

Bessie. Oh, no; that might not be right; and whether right or wrong, I shall be sure to get a beating if it is known. [*A voice calls Bessie.*] Oh dear, that is Sally! Let me go!

Alma. What a virago she must be, to inspire you with such fear; here is my address. [*Gives her a card.*] Think over what I have told you; then if you desire to place yourself under the care of my friend, apply to me at once, and I will assist you.

Bessie. I am very grateful, sir. [*A voice calls Bessie.*] Oh dear! if that isn't papa. Run, sir, please run; or I shall be beaten.

Alma. Farewell then, little bird-charmer. [*Aside.*] I'll hasten home and take a sketch from memory.　　[*Exit.*

Enter JOHN DIKEMAN.

John. What are you doing here, you lazy little good-for-nothing, idling away your time when we are waiting for dinner.　　[*Grasps her.*

Bessie. Oh, papa, please don't beat me; I only stopped a moment to rest and sing.

John. I'll teach you to sing a different song; that I will. [*Horn sounds; enter workmen.*] You go to dinner, boys, while I flog the gal!

[*Exit John, dragging Bessie after him.*

1st Workman. The brute! The hard-hearted old curmudgeon! He deserves to be raw-hided himself!

2d Workman. I say, let's do it, boys, if he ever lays hands on her again.

All. Agreed; we'll be ready for him.

1st Workman. He abuses his wife too, boys, and a smarter or prettier woman warn't to be found in these diggin's than she when he married her.

All. We'll lick him for that too.　　[*Horn sounds.*

1st Workman. Blow your old horn and be hanged to you, you old miser; we'll show you how it feels to be cudgelled, if you don't let that poor gal alone.

[*Exit all.*

SCENE II.—*Village Green; Mercy knitting under a tree.*

Enter BESSIE.

Bessie. Dear Mercy, I'm so glad to see you once more.
[*Embrace.*

Mercy. And haven't I been watching for you this whole long week? Glad to see me, truly; but you look sad, dearest. Pray what is the matter?

· *Bessie.* Only the same old story of father's injustice and Sally's cruelty.

Mercy. Poor child! but this shall not continue. I will speak to my father or Parson Beverly to-night.

Bessie. [*Shaking her head.*] It will do no good; any interference only subjects me to greater cruelty.

Yesterday I was sent to fetch a stray cow from the forest, when, who should I meet, but the very beautifulest young man I ever put my eyes upon; he asked me my name and all sort of questions.

Mercy. Had you never seen him before?

Bessie. No, and I never expect to again; he told me I could make a fine singer if I would practice; and he gave me his own name on a card; but Sally found it out and I had to destroy it to keep it from her; then I got such a beating from papa that I can scarcely move.

Mercy. Poor, poor child! if I could only tell Mr. Beverly.

Bessie. It would only draw the chains tighter about me. If I could only go to New York and learn to sing well enough to earn my own living by my voice.

Mercy. [*Clasping her hands and looking horrified.*] Don't think of going away off to that awful city. Why, Bessie, it's one of the very wickedest places that ever was known, except Sodom in the Bible. I've heard pa and the gentlemen that have been there say so. They always hurry away just as soon as they get their business done, for fear they will be waylaid and murdered.

Bessie. Well, well; quiet your fears, dear Mercy, I didn't say *I* intended to go; tho' I don't believe all they say about the city being so very wicked; and as to the gentlemen all hurrying away—it's no such a thing. There's parson Beverly always goes to Barnum's Museum when he's down to attend the Tract Society meetings. I've heard him say so myself, and he's a good, pious man, I'm sure, but I must go.

Mercy. Pray don't go, darling Bessie—at least not till you have sung that favorite melody of mine.

[*Bessie sings, standing with her bonnet in her hand; Mercy, affected to tears, covers her face.*

Bessie. [*Aside.*] She little thinks this is our last meeting. [*Will Littlefield approaches.*] Bless me, there comes that clown Will. [*Exit Bessie.*

[*Will Littlefield, with straw hat filled with apples, advances cautiously to Mercy's side and pours them at her feet.*

Mercy. [*Jumping.*] Oh my! Will! how you did frighten me!

Will. Did I ? Well, then, I'll take it all back !

Mercy. But where is Bessie ?

Will. Gone home, of course, as any sensible girl would, [*Aside*] leaving the field clear to me. [*To Mercy.*] You see, Mercy, I've brought you a few of our golden sweets —come clear over here on purpose.

Mercy. [*Selecting one.*] Yes, I see, Will, but you don't expect me to eat all these, I hope.

Will. I reckoned you'd stow away considerable of a pile, but that ain't neither here nor there, Mercy ; so pitch in and don't be bashful.

Mercy. You're a clever fellow, Will, and no mistake : how is your mother and the deacon ?

Will. The deacon, he's tolerable ; but the old woman's enjoyin' a terrible cold. I say, Mercy, wouldn't you like to pop down to Johnson's to a quilting frolic to-night.

Mercy. Thank you, Will ; but don't think I can make it convenient.

Will. Aren't sot agin sich things as quiltin' bees and apple parin's and the like, just because you've jined the church, are you ?

Mercy. No, Will !

Will. Maybe you don't like it because I took Sall Dikeman out to Baymount last 4th July ?

Mercy. On the contrary, I was pleased with it—hope you'll favor her with your company again.

Will. Not by a darned sight. The fact of the business is, I came down here, Mercy, to ax you ; but taking the percussion to peep through the window before rappin', who should I see but a tall, dandified, chap sittin' so concerned close to you, a jabbering away and casting sheep's eyes so mighty often at you, that I curlapsed, I did, and in mighty short order tu.

Mercy. Oh, that was only Cousin Joe.

Will. Maybe ; but it looked like purty darned warm cousening to me ; I s'pose you wouldn't have gone if I'd spunked up and asked you ?

Mercy. No !

Will. Sure you don't feel hurt, nor nothin', at my askin' Sall ?

Mercy. No, no ! not in the least.

Will. Fact is, Mercy, every fellow in town is in love

with you up tu the very brim, and you know it tu; if
you du look so down-kind-uv-cast, but there aren't one in
the whole posse of 'em that loves you as I du.

Mercy. Indeed?

Will. No indeed! When I see you a comin' intu
meetin', a lookin' so modest like, with them pink ribbins
a flutterin' about your pinker cheeks, I feel just as if you
was a big hunk of maple sugar, and I could swallow you
at one gob.   [*Opens his mouth.*

Mercy. [*Jumping back a pace or two.*] Oh, don't,
Will!

Will. I love you well enough to eat you up, but I'm
not a'goin' tu du it yet, so don't be scared. You see,
Mercy, our folks want me to get married and take the
farm; so I reckon it will suit them if we manage to hitch
hosses 'bout Christmas. [*Chucks her under the chin.*]
What do you say to that?

Mercy. [*Rising with dignity.*] I say no, sir!

Will. No?

Mercy. No!

  [*Will puckers up his face and makes a doleful attempt to cry as he sees Mercy start for home.*

Will. I say, Mercy, it's too bad for you to go trottin' off
in this kind of style when I come over on purpose to tell
you——

Mercy. Why, Will, I thought you came over on purpose to bring me golden sweets.

Will. And I know of some gals as would consider me
a golden sweet.

Mercy. Indeed!

Will. Yes, indeed: now you just wait and hear the
nub of the story, Mercy, and I reckon you'll change your
mind.

Mercy. No, Will, not if your story has forty nubs.

Will. [*Puckers up his face.*] Boo, hoo, hoo!

Mercy. [*Aside.*] Poor foolish fellow! I'm truly sorry
for him, but there is no help for it. [*Walks off a few
paces, turns.*] I say, Will!

Will. [*Peering out from under his arm, aside.*] She'll
have me yet, I'll bet a grist of dad's best wheat. [*Walks
up to Mercy.*] What is it, Mercy, darling; you see I'm
a poor heart-broken critter— boo! hoo! hoo!

Mercy. [*Extending her hand.*] I only wanted to say
we had better part friends.

Will. [*Taking her hand and examining it curiously.*]
Yes, Mercy, it's jest what I'd like. Maybe you'll pop
down to the quilting with me, if it's only to let folks know
I haven't got the mitten!

Mercy. Well, I will go with you just for once; but you
mustn't come bothering me again with your invitations.

Will. Mercy, you're right down clever! [*Aside.*] By
Jupiter! I'll get her yet!

Mercy. Good-day, Will!

Will. 'Spect I must say good-by if you're bent on goin'.
I shall be on hand bright and early for the quilting, so be
ready in season.   [*Exit both.*

SCENE III.—*Drawing-room in residence of Deacon Wilde.
Mercy engaged in sewing.*

Enter MRS. WILDE, *all in a flurry.*

Mrs. W. Sakes alive, Mercy, there's somebody coming
up the lane. I declare I can't imagine who it is! Do get
up and see if you know him. [*A rap.*] There! goodness
me; if he hasn't rapp'd! and here I am in my soiled apron
and rumpled cap! Do, Mercy, child, go and open the door
while I fix up. [*Mercy opens the door, while Mrs. Wilde,
at the extremity of the room, smooths her apron and cap,
and adjusts her glasses.*

Enter ALMA. MERCY *bows and offers a chair.*

Mrs. W. Yes, sit down, do.

Alma. Thank you; I am most happy to avail myself of
your kind offer.

Mercy. [*Aside.*] What eyes! *What hair!*

Mrs. W. You look fatigued, sir; have you travelled far?

Alma. No, madam; I am stopping at present in your
village; being by profession an artist I wish to sketch
some of the fine views hereabouts, but I find poor accommodations at the hotel.

Mrs. W. Maxwell keeps a miserable place, that is true.

Enter RACHEL SNOW; *looks inquisitively at the artist.*
1*

Rachel. Good mornin', Miss Wilde; good mornin', Mercy! I didn't know you'd got a *man* here, or I wouldn't have come in.

Mrs. W. Why, Rachel, I thought that was what brought you over.

Rachel. I reckon you've took to judgin' others by yourself. 'Spect you're goin' to have your pictures painted, bein' you've got the artist here.

Mrs. W. Law me! aren't you the very one that's been paintin' the 'squire's picture?

Alma. Yes, ma'am; the same. [*Aside; looking at Mercy.*] Could I but transfer the beauty of your face to canvas, I should be the happiest of men. [*To Mrs. W.*] If you will direct me, madam, to some private family, where I may obtain a room for a studio, with board and lodging, I shall be exceedingly grateful.

Mrs. W. There's our spare chamber, which is never in use at this season, and plenty of room at the table, if you will accept.

Alma. I shall be only too happy.

Rachel. I was going to say, sir, you might find better accommodations at my brother's, perhaps, but I s'pose it's of no use now.

Alma. Since this lady has been so kind as to offer, I am only too happy to accept. Perhaps, when you see my work, madam, you may be inclined to give me something to do—that young lady's portrait, for instance.

[*Pointing to Mercy.*

Mrs. W. That's the very subject Justice and I was talking over last night. Says I to the deacon, says I, "You're getting old, and there'll never be a better time for you to have your picture painted." You see we'd been over tu Squire Kendrick's examining theirs. "That's all true enough, and I want yours," says he. "Then there's Mercy, just as handsome as a picture, and we shall both want hers," says I. "Yes, and she will want both of ours," says he; so you see you'll be likely to get a fair job— that is, if you're reasonable.

Alma. You shall set your own price, ma'am.

Mrs. W. Then it's a bargain, and you may move your tools over right away.

Rachel. [*Tossing her head. Aside.*] There's other folks

in the village, I reckon, besides the Wildes. [*To Mrs. Wilde.*] I 'spect there won't be any chance for any one else to get pictures, now you are going into it by the wholesale.

Mrs. W. That's as you and this gentleman can agree.

Alma. [*Aside.*] Heaven protect me if I have her phiz to paint.

To Mrs. W. I will hasten my return, that I may commence immediately on your portraits. [*A low bow to Mercy. Exit Alma, Rachel Snow following closely at his heels.*

Alma. [*Aside.*] Aye, a smiling Providence brings me to dwell with an angel! Such beauty, such angelic loveliness!

Rachel. Was you speaking of me, sir?

Alma. You? The dev——. I beg pardon. No, ma'am.

Rachel. 'Spect the Wildes will try to make you think there aren't anybody else of any consequence in town. Good-day, sir!

Alma. Good-day [*Aside*], and a long absence, I pray you!

Mercy. Dear mother, isn't he a splendid-looking young man?

Mrs. W. He wants shavin' terribly! I can't tell how he would look with that black beard off. I shall offer him the deacon's razor when he comes, for I guess he must have lost his'n!

Mercy. Why, mamma, it's all the fashion for the gentlemen to wear mustachios and the like.

Mrs. W. And a mighty foolish fashion it is, according to my ideas. I'd like to see your pa going around like a monkey, with a bushel of hair on his face, just because it's the fashion!

Scene IV.—*Quilting Party.—A large room.*

Enter WILL LITTLEFIELD *and* MERCY, MARK KENDRICK, LOWBURY, WETHERBE, LETHRIDGE, RACHEL SNOW, *and villagers generally. An old man sits in the corner, flourishing now and then a red silk handkerchief.*

Mark. [*With quilt in his hand.*] Come on, boys and

girls, let's give it a shake. [*All gather around, shake the quilt, fold it, and then prepare for a dance.*

Will. Come, who's for the dance? [*Catches Mercy, and leads her out; form for Danish polka. All except Rachel and old man dance.*

Rachel. [*Tossing her head as she goes to the old man.*] Ah, how my heart aches to see these young people indulge in such frivolous amusements.

Old man. Heart aches because you didn't get asked to join, Rachel.

Rachel. It's no such a thing. Do you s'pose I'd dance? I, a member of the church! No. There's Mercy Wilde settin' a poor example to the world's people; but, thank heaven, it ain't me.

Old man. Yes, that Mercy's a likely gal, as was her mother before her: a master pretty girl was Maggie; cut you out with Justice too, Rachel, but you mustn't hold a grudge against her, for that's worse than dancing.

Rachel. [*Aside.*] Must that be ever thrown in my face? Never, never will I forgive her! [*To old man.*] You forget, dadda, I never would have married Justice Wilde; no, no more than I would join in the sinful pleasure of dancing to-night.

Mercy. [*To Will Littlefield.*] The lynx eyes of Rachel Snow are following me. No doubt she will go to Parson Beverly with a high-sounding tale of my frivolity.

Will. Never fear, Rachel—I'll fix her; trust me for that. [*Will walks up to Rachel.* [*Aside.*] Deuce take the ugly old mischief-maker.

[*To Rachel.*] I say, Rachel, give me your hand for the next dance?

Rachel. My dear William, I feel more like weeping than dancing. Don't you feel——

Will. Yes, amazingly like joining in this quadrille. Dancing is a healthy recreation, approved of by the Church. [*Catches her waist and goes whirling off in a waltz with her.*

Rachel. Why, William, my dear William, you're crazy.

Will. Not I. I always said you were built for a dancer. Aunt Rachel, isn't this glorious fun, now?

[*Leads Rachel to the old man and joins Mercy.*

Will. Let her prate now if she pleases.

Mercy. I am under great obligations to you, Will, for extricating me from that unpleasant dilemma.

Will. [*Aside.*] She's coming around, sure as preachin'. I'll get the handsome critter yet!

[*Exit all but Rachel and Will.*

Rachel. You know, William, that I feel a great interest in you, don't you, dear?

Will. Is that so?

Rachel. Yes, a very great interest in you!

Will. You're a clever critter, Rachel!

Rachel. I feel a very great interest indeed in you; and I think if you would just leave off running around after that Mercy Wilde, and look up some good smart girl, that would make you a good wife.

Will. I shall never marry Mercy Wilde, Rachel, for a very good reason.

Rachel. I'm glad to hear you say that, Will; it sounds like coming to your senses. There are a plenty of good, substantial girls that would marry a good-lookin', well-to-do chap like you; in fact, I may say I know of one.

Will. You're joking, Rachel, I know.

Rachel. Not a bit, William, dear.

Will. [*Aside, rolling his eyes.*] William, dear! Lord, help me!

Rachel. I know you deserve a kind, affectionate wife; and it e'enamost breaks my heart to see you so alone. I—I—know of one, but I suppose it wouldn't be proper for a young woman—

Will. [*Aside, fanning himself with his hat.*] Young woman! By Jemima! I shall faint after that!

Rachel. Like me to speak out in plain words.

Will. [*Looking frightened.*] Lord, save us! Perhaps it wouldn't.

Rachel. [*Edging towards Will, who edges off.*] Dear William! Can't you think of somebody you know who would make a loving, affectionate wife? You can, I know! There's a dear man. [*Puts him under the chin.*

Will. What kind of looking critter is she?

Rachel. She looks like—like—oh, I can't, William.

Will. Then don't!

Rachel. [*Throwing herself in his arms.*] It's me, William.

Will. [*Pushing her away.*] Get out! Get out!
[*Exit Will.*

Rachel. The ungrateful wretch! But that's just the way
with all the men. I am resolved after this never to
marry—never, never! In blessed singleness I'll pass my
days!

Scene V.—*Room in John Dikeman's cottage.—Mrs.
Dikeman sits rocking a cradle, has a baby in her arms.
John Dikeman occupies the opposite side of the room;
two or three farm-boys around the table, on which is a
mug of cider.*

John. At the age of twenty-one, boys, I run in debt
for this 'ere farm, and I married Miss Dikeman, there,
for I expected she'd turn in and help me pay for it. I
can't say but what she did well enough for a year or two;
but after that she began to run behind. Now we've been
married eighteen year, coming this January, and she's
had twelve children, a thing I didn't expect of her; but
then she never did consider. [*Baby cries.*] You jist stop
that youngern's mouth, will you, Miss Dikeman? [*Drinks
from the mug.*] Folks used to say my wife was the
smartest woman in town; but I haven't seen much of it
late years, and a mighty disappintment it's been to me,
too; but what can you expect of a woman that never
considers. [*Baby cries.*] Miss Dikeman, do you want me
to tell you agin to stop that youngern's mouth? [*Both
babies cry. Mrs. Dikeman seizes the baby in the cradle
and rushes out of the room.*] I've told her often enough
she must have quiet children; but she will persist in
having the noisiest youngerns in town, just to have her
own way I s'pose. [*Drinks. Exit boys. Clock strikes
eleven.*] Eleven o'clock! I declare; high time we were all
of us in bed; I hope Miss Dikeman'll have sense enough
not to let that youngern squall all night and keep me
awake. [*Exit John.*

Enter Bessie *with hat and shawl on, and bundle in her
hand.*

Bessie. All gone at last, leaving the way clear for me;
Poor mamma! how pale and worn she looked as I passed
her door! Oh, that I could take her with me, far away

from the tyrant who dishonors the name of husband and father. But it cannot be; innocent little ones need her care. If, in thus leaving home, I am doing wrong, may Heaven forgive. It is impossible for me to remain here longer and live. The blows of a father, the taunts and insults of a sister, I can bear no longer. The words of the kind stranger whom I met in the wood have awakened in my heart a desire to be something more than a menial. Yes; I will seek for the great Baratoli. Though I have lost the address of the young man who promised me aid, I will not despair, neither do I go out into the wide world alone. A kind, protecting Providence is still over me to guard, guide, and cheer me on my lonely pilgrimage. Farewell, parents, brothers, sisters all. Though I find an humbler shelter, may I be blessed with more love.

ACT II.

SCENE I.—*A dark cave lit by torches.—Table in the centre, with bottles, glasses, and cards.—Maxwell, Lethridge, and Wetherbe sit round the table.*

Wetherbe. [*Shuffling the cards.*] Which shall it be, boys, euchre or seven up?

Lethridge. Neither! I'm disgusted with three-hand games. Denville Lowbury is ripe for gathering, and he must be brought in, boys.

Wetherbe. His love for Mercy Wilde has soft-soddered him, Lethridge. I tell you he is not fit for our kind of work.

Lethridge. Not a bit of it. I've had experience in that line myself. He'll come out all right.

Wetherbe. And so have I, captain, to my sorrow! Poor Annie. If she had listened to me I might have been— but—heigh-ho! [*Turns out a glass of brandy; drinks.*] 'Twon't do to moralize.

Lethridge. Annie is yours, this night, if you say so, Wetherbe.

Wetherbe. Pray, explain, most worthy captain of the Red!

Lethridge. Old Daniel Hart and his wife have gone ten
miles away to a camp-meeting, leaving Annie alone to
guard the premises and take care of her superannuated
grandpapa. Never were bolt or bar brought in use to
guard the door to Daniel Hart's cottage. Pull the bobbin
and the latch will fly up.

Wetherbe. Ah, you do not know her spirit. She will
resist, scream in true woman fashion, and rouse the old
man.

Lethridge. Gabriel's trump would scarcely rouse him;
he's as deaf as an adder; and as to resistance, I think my
strength, with yours, will be all-sufficient.

Wetherbe. But where shall I put her?

Lethridge. A cage is already prepared in the cavern
adjoining this. Annie is not the first fair one who has
found a resting-place there. The deacon's daughter may
ere long come to keep her company, provided Lowbury
throws the bait right.

Wetherbe. How? Explain yourself.

Lethridge. The girl will mitten Lowbury for the handsome artist, Alma; and in his desperation Lowbury will
come to me, as he has often done before, for sympathy;
I can easily draw him into our charmed circle by promis-
ing to snare his dove.

Wetherbe. Ah! I see, I see; let's drink to his health.
[*All drink.*

Lethridge. And that is not all I intend to accomplish.
I have a grudge against the pious old deacon to feed, and
in no way can I wound him so sorely as to kidnap his
handsome daughter. [*A noise outside; torches extin-
guished; table, men, chairs, and all disappear through
floor.*

SCENE II.—*Artist's studio at Deacon Wilde's.—Canvas,
papers, packing-boxes, and pictures scattered around.*

Enter MERCY WILDE.

Mercy. Alas, he's going, and 'tis Sarah who is driving
him away by her jealous freaks and whims. [*Discovers
Bessie's portrait.*] But what do I see! Dear, dear

Bessie! So true to life that it seems as if the full, ripe lips were about to address me. [*Enter Alma unperceived.*] How full of sorrow are those sweet, brown eyes! Oh, Bessie, darling child, whither are you wandering?

[*Kisses the picture.*

Alma. [*Aside.*] What a compliment to my talent. I wish I were a picture, and you served me thus, sweet Mercy!

Mercy. [*Gazing around.*] Alas, he is going, going—

[*Alma enters, Mercy screams.*

Alma. Be not frightened, dearest Mercy, at my sudden appearance.   [*Takes her hand.*

Mercy. Let me go, please.

Alma. No, never again, till I have told you how dear you have grown to this poor heart of mine; never, never again, till I tell you all my love—till I tell you how, in seeking to portray the physical beauty of your face, I caught a gleam of the spiritual. I saw your soul's beauty shining through all, illuminating every feature, giving you that monetary beauty, that radiant expression, which took my poor heart captive. Mercy, darling, tell me, have I loved in vain? [*Mercy rests her head upon his shoulder. He steals his arm around her.*]

Enter DEACON WILDE *with pipe in his mouth, unperceived.* ALMA *kisses* MERCY.

Deacon Wilde. There, there, Alma, guess that'll do. I vow, if I don't believe you're better at kissing the gals than painting portraits!

Alma. Excuse me, sir, but I was going to speak to you about your daughter. I—that is—to say

Deacon W. Ha, ha, ha! Yes, I understand just how that is—been there myself—stuttered and stammered worse than you do, too; ha! ha! ha!

Alma. Do you give your consent? May I hope?

Deacon W. I rather like your spirit, young man, but there's one hitch in the machine. You are not a Christian —that is to say, of our sort.

Alma. But I'll unite with your church.

Deacon W. Not so fast; we want the genuine article— that is to say, the Simon pure—when we have a Christian. Now, I dare say, you don't even know the creed you're so ready to subscribe to.

Alma. But Mercy can teach it to me, and I'll swear to believe every word.

Deacon W. Swearin' is against the rules of the church —don't allow it, no how. [*To Mercy.*] I s'pose Massa, you've been just silly enough to fall in love with this fellow, and if I don't say yes to his suit, you'll break your heart over it.

Mercy. I'm afraid I shall.

Deacon W. I s'pose your going to make a six months' journey to London with them pictures of yours.

Alma. Yes, sir; and I want the assurance of your approbation before I leave. Your consent to our union— however distant the happy day—will help to make my journey abroad endurable.

Deacon W. [*Handing him a pocket Bible.*] There, take that with you, and study it carefully in your absence. If in six months' time you return to us with the right heart, the right spirit, and still love my daughter as she deserves to be loved—why, she's yours; and now Heaven bless you, my boy.   [*Exit deacon.*

Alma. [*Placing ring on Mercy's finger.*] Keep this little circlet, dear Mercy, till I return, as an emblem of my love.

Mercy. But why go at all, dearest Alma?

Alma. I go that I may win both fame and a fortune— to lay at your feet, love. I have two magnificent pictures —one, *par excellence*, which must be exhibited at the Crystal Palace in London. I challenge the world to produce its equal—look you! [*Alma draws aside a covering and exhibits the portrait of Mercy.*]

Mercy. It is indeed beautiful, but not at all like me.

Alma. It is supremely beautiful, and very like you. [*Horn sounds.*] There goes that confounded stage-horn, and I'm not half ready. [*Kisses Mercy, then commences packing, flies first to one thing, then another; Mercy endeavors to help him. Horn sounds again. Catches Mercy by the waist and kisses her as he passes to strap a box; rolls up a parcel. Horn sounds third time. Drops parcel, gives Mercy a desperate hug. Stage-driver and Deacon Wilde appear in the door.*]

Deacon. Come, come, young man, passengers grumbling outside.

Alma. Yes, sir, ready in just one minute.

[*Kisses Mercy again.   Exit all.*

Enter Mrs. Wilde. *Attempts to put things to rights. Goes to the window and calls.*

Justice! I say, Justice, you come in here and help me move this big box. A pretty looking place this for a spare chamber, and company coming to-night.

Enter Deacon Wilde.

Deacon. Well, Maggie, he's off at last, and I s'pose Massa'll spend the rest of the day in crying.

Mrs. W. Yes, I s'pose so. Well, he is a nice kind of a chap is Mr. Alma; at first I didn't like all that brush around his mouth, but I don't mind it so much now.

Deacon W. Don't you think, Maggie, that we ought to tell her just how she came to us, and all about it?

Mrs. W. Deary me! Justice, are you crazy? Tell her? No, it would be the death of her; indeed it would!

Deacon W. It's been on my mind for a long time, and it troubles me, Maggie! Surely, she is old enough now to be told what we know.

Mrs. W. She never need to know anything about it. It can do her no good, Justice; not the least; so please keep your tongue in your mouth.   [*Exit both.*

Scene III.—*New York.—Drawing-room in house of Baratoli.*

Enter Bessie, *with dusting brush, followed by* Madam Baratoli.

Madam B. Now, child, see that everything is properly arranged and dusted, for Madam Elva, the celebrated prima donna, is to return from the opera with Pauline and the Seignior.

Bessie. [*Courtesies.*] Yes, ma'am. [*Exit Madam B.*] Yes, here I am at last; a servant in the mansion of the great Baratoli. When his rich, full tones fall on my ear, he little dreams how they thrill my heart. Oh that I could see the stranger who first mentioned his name to me; I would fall at his feet and bless him. Though a servant, a menial, there is affection for me here; even the high-born Madam looks kindly on me, and Baratoli is

pleasant and courteous to all. But I must to my practice; ha! they little dream Brown Bessie's fingers sweep
the pearl keys of the grand piano. It may be wrong,
but I can't resist the temptation. [*Sits down and exe-
cutes a simple air. While she is playing the door softly
opens, and Baratoli enters in dressing-gown and slippers.
As Bessie concludes the song he advances.*

Baratoli. My sweet warbler, pray tell me who you
are?

Bessie. Forgive, oh, forgive me, sir. [*Attempts to kneel
at his feet; he raises her and takes her hand.*

Baratoli. Don't be frightened, child. Pray tell me
who you are, and where you learned to sing so sweetly.

Bessie. Oh, sir, I came from the country, far away. I
was taught to sing by the birds of the forest; I used
often to run away from home to the wood—for my father
did not love me—and I would sometimes sing for hours
with only the birds to listen. One day a huntsman
passing by chanced to hear my voice, and he told me of
you; so I started from home alone to find you. But I
thought, on reaching this great, noisy city, I should never
be able to make you out; and when I did at last reach
your mansion I was frightened by the splendor about me.
I trembled when I beheld you, and I dared not make my
wishes known; so I became a servant here, that I might
feast my soul with the music of your voice.

Baratoli. And what is your name?

Bessie. Brown Bessie; they said they gave me that
name because I was so brown and ugly.

Baratoli. Ugly, with those large, hazel eyes? You are
splendid, Bessie; henceforth you are my pupil. Your
untaught melody has instructed me.

Enter MADAM BARATOLI, ELVA, *and* PAULINE.

Welcome, friends; by remaining at home I have found
a prodigy; now I can show you what I mean by natural
execution. [*Looks of envy pass between Pauline and
Elva.*] Sit down, child, and give us one of your simple
melodies. [*Bessie sings.*]

Baratoli. You see her style is easy, natural, and grace-
ful; if willing, we may all be taught of her! [*Leads*

Bessie to his mother.] To you, my dear mother, I consign her; let her be provided with everything necessary for her comfort; she is henceforth my pupil.

Madam. Come, darling! I hope my son will not be disappointed in you. You have a fine voice, but it needs cultivation.

Bessie. I'll try my best to succeed, indeed I will!

[*Exit Madam B., Baratoli, and Bessie.*

Pauline. A protégée, indeed; another silly freak of my uncle's.

Elva. Ay, well may you frown. She is destined to supplant you, both in your uncle's purse and his affection.

Pauline. And you in the heart of the public and the love of Baratoli! ha! ha! Look to your own laurels, my dear!

Elva. [*Clenching her hands.*] She shall not live to see that day! I will invoke the powers of Satan to destroy her!

Pauline. By my soul, Elva, you have a countenance fitted to do the devil's work. I wish you success!

Elva. And you a coward's heart; not too good to wish evil, but too weak, too womanish to execute!

Pauline. Thanks! We appreciate each other.

SCENE IV.—*London, 1850.— Picture gallery of the Crystal Palace.—Portraits of Mercy Wilde and Brown Bessie.—Alma stands beside a policeman, who fastens a placard, " Not for sale," on the portrait of Mercy.*

Alma. There, that will do! I think now we shall be less annoyed by purchasers.

Enter LEDYARD THORRINGTON *and* JACK HINTON, *arm in arm,* JACK *pointing to portrait of* MERCY.

Jack. I say, there's a beauty for you, Ledyard!

Ledyard. [*Aside.*] Great Heavens, my cousin Constance. [*To policeman.*] Who owns that painting?

Police. That gentleman, over there, sir [*pointing to Alma*]; but hit's not for sale!

Ledyard. By gay prince Hal, but I'll have it! [*Addresses Alma.*] Is yonder fine specimen from life, sir?

Alma. It is!

Ledyard. And the original, is she of English birth?

Alma. No, sir, she is American!

Ledyard. May I ask——

Alma. I feel myself at liberty to say nothing farther, sir. [*Turns away.*] What surly dogs the English are!

Ledyard. What unmannerly pups the Americans are!

Police. [*Drawing Ledyard aside.*] Hi say, sir, what would you give to learn the whereabouts of yon lady in the frame?

Ledyard. A five-pound note!

Police. Hit's ha bargain. Step this way, sir!

Ledyard. Proceed, old cock, I'm listening.

Police. Not till hi've seen the color of the chink!

Ledyard. Here, you rascal. [*Drops a piece of gold in his hand.*] Now proceed, or I'll take the kinks out of you devilish quick!

Police. Her name is Mercy Wilde, the daughter of a yeoman living hin the town of Halderly, State of Massasoit, continent hov Hamerica!

Ledyard. [*Putting it down in memorandum book.*] Are you sure you're correct, old cock?

Police. Hi ad it from im as owns the picture!

Old GENTLEMAN *enters, and walks towards the picture.*

Ledyard. By Jupiter! if there isn't uncle Tom, walking straighter than I've seen him these ten years. If he gets his eye on that picture I'm undone, or done up! [*To police.*] I say, old chap, you just hover around and hear what passes between my uncle and that dog of an artist. I'll pay you well!

Police. Thanks, generous stranger; hime hall hattention!

Jack. What 'pon earth is in the wind now, old boy? At first I could scarcely get you into the picture-gallery at all, and now you are ready to give your fortune to possess the portrait of a country girl whom nobody knows or cares to know.

Ledyard. Listen, Jack, while I a tale unfold. You

know my uncle Tom, there, once had a daughter, Constance.

Jack. I have heard as much.

Ledyard. Well, she made a runaway match with a poor scapegrace of a music-teacher named Ayelton. My uncle succeeded in separating them, and carried my cousin away to America. I suppose the separation broke her heart, for she died soon after giving birth to a daughter, and, as the story goes, the daughter died with her; but that part of it I will swear is false: for yon picture is a regular Thorrington, as much like the portrait of my cousin Constance, that hangs in Eildon Hall, as though it was painted from it. My uncle will say the same. He will search for the original, and if she is found, as the next heir, comes in ahead of me for my uncle's property.

Jack. Ah! I see. But what can you do?

Ledyard. But for that graceless scamp of an artist I would have had it out of my uncle's way. Now there is nothing for me to do but to watch his moves, and be before him in whatever he undertakes. I've got the policeman on the scent. You follow them up, too, Jack, and hear what you can. [*Jack steps near Thomas Thorrington and Alma.*

Thomas. It's like seeing her again, my precious, precious Constance!

Alma. Calm yourself, sir. The original cannot be your granddaughter. I know her parents well—plain country people, of American birth.

Thomas. But I tell you it is my Constance's child. That Thorrington face convinces me of it. You look incredulous; but listen, sir. I had a daughter, only and well beloved. She married without my knowledge. I, in my wrath, separated her from her husband, and took her to America. She died while I was absent from her; for, having fallen ill of fever in New York, my wife left her to the care of her nurse, and came to attend upon me. She died, and we were told the infant died also, and was buried with her in a quiet country village in Massachusetts. I did not go to ascertain the facts of the case, but returned, heart-broken, home to England. That picture causes me to doubt the death of the child. I cannot die, I cannot even rest, till I am satisfied.

Alma. I shall soon return to America, and, if you see fit to accompany me, will assist you as far as I am able in clearing up the mystery; though I am satisfied you are wrong in your suppositions.

Thomas. Thanks for your generous offer. I shall avail myself of it. [*Aside.*] Oh, that I might find the daughter, and restore her to the place her mother once held in my heart! On my knees would I ask forgiveness for the wrongs done her poor mother. [*Exit Thomas.*

Jack. You were right, Ledyard: he too sees a Thorrington likeness, and is away with the artist on a wild-goose chase to America, as soon as the fair closes.

Ledyard. I must be before him in this business. What say you to a trip across the Atlantic, Jack? I must secure the damsel before he gets wind of her whereabouts.

Jack. Just the thing for me, Ledyard: you know I am fond of adventure; but if you succeed in securing the beauty, what will you do with her?

Ledyard. Put her out of my good uncle's way, or perhaps the safest plan will be to marry her myself, if she is as handsome as the cross-grained artist represents. Then I shall make sure of the fortune, whether my uncle will or no.

Jack. Good! I'm in for it. When do we set out?

Ledyard. As soon as I can make the governor shell out. Won't he blow though, when I go in for another hundred! Come, let's be off, now that the thing is settled. [*Exit Jack and Ledyard.*

Alma [*To Policeman.*] That portrait must bear a remarkable likeness to the old gentleman's daughter, judging from his appearance.

Police. A singular circumstance, very.

Alma. Perhaps he may be insane on the subject of his daughter's marriage, and so fancies the portrait like her.

Police. Hi thought has much myself; but has true has hi live, there's another struck dumb with the picture! [*Points to Ayelton, who, having caught a glimpse of the portrait, turns pale and leans against the wall for support.*] Hi say, hit beats the devil, hit does!

Ayelton. Yes, it is her face, her angel face, that I have been searching for years in vain!

Alma. [*Approaching.*] Of whom are you speaking?

Ayelton. Of Constance, my wife; pray, sir, tell me where I may find her.

Alma. [*Aside.*] The same name. By Heaven, I begin to doubt my own senses!

Ayelton. Oh, sir; for seventeen years I have been separated from her. Have you no pity?

Alma. But this is a young lady, an American, scarce seventeen years of age; so she cannot be the lost Constance whom you seek. [*Aside.*] His mind must be wandering!

Ayelton. True, true, but it may be our child; and I hear my Constance had a daughter, though I was never permitted to see her. But they told me both were dead! Oh, sir; if you have a heart akin to pity, pray tell me where she may be found!

Alma. She is the daughter of plain American people. I came across her in my rambles for sketches of American scenery. Her surpassing loveliness attracted my eye, and I painted her portrait, little thinking it would create the sensation it has here.

Ayelton. Do you know her parents?

Alma. Yes; honest country people!

Ayelton. Does she, this beauty, resemble them in looks or appearance?

Alma. Not in the least; in fact, there is quite a contrast!

Ayelton. [*Drawing a locket from his bosom.*] Look you here. [*Alma looks and starts at the likeness.*] Oh! you see the resemblance.

Alma. Yes, they are surprisingly alike; but then such circumstances have happened before.

Ayelton. [*Leading Alma aside.*] Listen to me for a few moments and I will give you a brief sketch of my life. I was poor! The parents of Constance were wealthy. We saw each other, loved, and were clandestinely married. The truth, however, could not long be concealed. While absent in London preparing a home for my bride, her parents left England, taking her forcibly with them. Imagine my anguish—my desperation—on returning to Eildon Hall to find it closed, and no clue left by which I might find my wife. Two years I spent on the Conti-

2

nent, searching in every town and hamlet for Constance, but in vain. At the end of that time I received news of the return of the Thorringtons to England. I sought the stern parents and demanded my wife; but they told me that my wife and child had died abroad; farther than this, I could elicit nothing; even the privilege of weeping over their graves was denied me. Do you, can you wonder that I cursed Thomas Torrington to his face as the destroyer of my happiness?

Alma. He, too, has noticed the picture which so resembles your lost Constance.

Ayelton. He! has he been here, and what did he say? I charge you, as you hope for happiness, to tell me the truth!

Alma. He confesses to having lost a daughter in America. The nurse in attendance represented that the child died also; but it seems he was not a witness of the fact. He, like you, labors under the delusion that the child is living. He is to accompany me to America on my return, and ascertain the facts.

Ayelton. But he shall not rob me of my child! Is it not enough that he killed my wife?

Alma. Should the young lady prove his granddaughter—a thing quite impossible in my opinion—he only proposes to restore her to her rights.

Ayelton. She will not care for his rights. Thanks to a kind Providence, I have now a fortune of my own, and through the magnanimity of our noble-hearted Queen, for a trifling service rendered the crown, I can claim a title superior to the Thorringtons. But my life, what has it been but one long, dreary day of wretchedness? To find a daughter, grown to womanhood, the image of my Constance, would indeed be as salve to my lacerated heart.

Alma. [*Hands him a card.*] That, sir, is the address of the young lady—the original of the portrait—with the route you are to journey accurately noted. You can seek her, and learn the truth from her own lips.

Ayelton. A thousand thanks, my kind friend! You, too, think I may be successful?

Alma. No, sir; candidly, I cannot give you the slightest encouragement to hope. You will perhaps be better satisfied to visit her humble home and converse with her parents.   [*Exit both.*

Scene V.—*Musical Rehearsal.—Madam Elva's House.*
—Drawing-room.

Enter Elva, Madam Baratoli, Pauline, Bessie, Seignior Baratoli, *Musical Critics, Guests, &c.*

Pauline. [*Aside to Elva.*] Have you spoken to Jones
and Barton?

Elva. Yes; and the reporters for the daily papers.
They have all promised to cut the performance dead in
to-morrow's papers.

Pauline. Good! then the forward hussy will not get
so much as an encore.

Elva. Not she; they will treat her efforts with the
most cutting sarcasm. But remember, Pauline, she must
sleep in my house to-night. Help me to persuade her to
remain. Do you understand?

Pauline. Ay, and wish you success in your diabolical
scheme.

   [*Baratoli leads Bessie to the front; she sings. Re-
      ceives enthusiastic applause.*

Elva. [*Aside.*] Curses, curses on them. So this is the
way critics keep their word. This steels me to my purpose. This night she dies!

Madam B. Dear child; I congratulate you on your
success! Don't you see the seignior is in ecstasies. But
you look pale, darling!

Bessie. Only a little tired, that is all!

Baratoli. This exertion, after having attended the opera,
is too much for your nervous temperament, dear Bessie.
Let us go home at once!

Elva. Rather let her remain here and go quietly to
bed. I will see her well attended.

Baratoli. What say you, dear Bessie?

Bessie. As you please; only I would not like to incon-
venience Madam Elva.

Elva. [*Throwing her arm around her.*] What non-
sense is this? Come, good seignior, get you gone at once,
that we damsels may retire, and refresh ourselves by rest
for to-morrow night's great work.

Baratoli. So, so, you drive us away! Well, well! Good-
night, Bessie.   [*Madam B. kisses Bessie.*

[*Exit all except Bessie and Elva. Scene changes to bed-room.*

Elva. [*Pointing to a couch.*] There, dear Bessie, you will find a resting-place for the night. May your sleep be sweet and your dreams pleasant. Good-night! [*Aside.*] An eternal sleep be yours.

Bessie. Good-night, dear Elva. [*Exit Elva.*] What a delightful thing it is to be a great singer, to be sure! Such applause! But the most gratifying of all was to see the good seignior look so well pleased. Oh! I never was so happy in all my life, I'm sure! I must write to darling Mercy and tell her all about it; she will scarcely believe her senses; and I shall be a prima donna at last. I fancy Madam Elva does not like me; perhaps she thinks I may win laurels from her; but I'm sure I have no wish to supplant her, and Pauline's brow was as dark as night. I tremble yet from the look she gave me. [*Goes to the window; looks out.*] Surely day is dawning and I have not had a wink of sleep. [*Throws herself on the couch. Elva approaches from outside, puts her head cautiously through the window.*

Elva. Let her say her prayers, for her fate is sealed.

[*Exit.*

Bessie. [*Springing from the bed.*] What a wicked child I have been, to be sure; to go to bed without first thanking Heaven for my success. The angels whispered in my ear, reminding me of my neglect. [*Kneels by couch. A heavy weight falls, crushing the bed. Bessie springs to her feet, clasps her hands.*] Saved, saved by my prayers, from a terrible death! Yes, Heaven, that has already made me the recipient of countless mercies, will protect me still from the machinations of the wicked.

ACT III.

SCENE 1.—*Forest and glen in Alderly, Massachusetts, near residence of Deacon Wilde.—Jack Hinton and Ledyard Thorrington have arrived, with design of kidnapping Mercy.—Enter arm in arm.*

Ledyard. Deuce take me, Jack, if I don't give up horses, dogs—ay, and even cards—for the little vixen.

Jack. Have you seen her?

Ledyard. Yes, and a splendid creature she is; carries a high head though. You ought to have seen the look of disdain the little gypsy gave me when I spoke to her. But what success have you met with?

Jack. Well, I reconnoitred at the farm; got the old woman by the gills before she knew what I was up to; and had the truth clean out of her in less time than I've been telling ye.

Ledyard. Now, you don't say, Jack.

Jack. You just listen, and don't interrupt. You see I went in with my pack to sell goods, and very quietly asked the old woman for the girl Mercy, whom they had been kind enough to take and bring up. You ought to have seen the color come and go in her truthful face. She didn't attempt to deny my assertion; owned up at once that the child was brought to their door in the night, and left in a basket on the steps; that they had brought her up as their own, and no one—not even their neighbors—suspected her of being a foundling.

Ledyard. So far so good; but have they no clue to the child's name or parentage?

Jack. None at all. There was nothing in the basket save a child's apparel and a few trinkets—so they have been able to learn nothing; but I was in hopes to get a glimpse of her myself, as the old woman told me she had come to the glen.

Ledyard. Good; let us remain and watch, for she must pass this way.   [*Secrete themselves.*

Jack. Hark! I hear steps. [*Denville Lowbury enters from one side as Mercy enters from the other.*

Mercy. Oh, Denville, is that you? You look troubled. I hope nothing has gone ill with you!

Denville. Mercy, I am despised and shunned. It is of no use for me to try to put on an air of respectability, for I meet with a cold shoulder from everybody.

Mercy. You are greatly in error, Denville. You have but to think and act as a man to be considered such!

Denville. [*Attempting to take her hand, which she withdraws.*] You, Mercy, and you alone can, if you will, bring me back to truth and right.

Mercy. I am willing to do all in my power for you,

Denville, but you must rely upon Heaven and your-self.

Denville. Will you marry me, Mercy? [*Grasping her hand.*

Mercy. Please release me, sir; that is asking too much.

Denville. [*Dropping her hand.*] Then I must sink lower, lower still. You, Mercy Wilde, hold the scales of my destiny. With you at my side, with your bright ex-ample to cheer me on in the right path, I might be hon-ored and respected.

Mercy. [*Shaking her head.*] It can never be!

Denville. Then I am lost, lost, lost! [*Exit Denville.*

Mercy. Poor youth, you have my sympathy, my pray-ers, but not my love—no, no; that is already given to an-other!

Enter DEACON WILDE.

Deacon. I thought I should find you here, Mercy. Here is a letter from your runaway friend, Bessie, I presume. It looks like her scribbling, and is post-marked New York; but wait a bit before you read it, for I have something I wish to say to you. Come, sit down on this log and rest a bit. [*Both sit down.*

Mercy. What is it, dear papa? [*Taking his hand.*]

Deacon. You see, I've got a kind of an idea in my head that I ought to tell you—should have made a clean breast of it before, but for Maggie; she says you'll take it to heart.

Mercy. What is it, dearest papa? Don't keep me in this suspense, but tell me at once!

Deacon. It's a bit of a story, child; so listen. Just seventeen years ago this very day, bright and early in the morning, Maggie and I were roused out of a sound sleep by a terrible clatter at the door. As soon as I could dress myself, and that warn't many minutes, I bounced out, and what should I find but a basket with a wee bit of a baby in it, and nobody to be seen.

Mercy. Why, papa, whose child was it, do you think?

Deacon. Oh, Mercy, that is the question Maggie and I have been asking ourselves every blessed day since.

Mercy. Oh, papa! you don't, no, you can't mean—
that——

Deacon. Yes, dearest Mercy, that baby was yourself,
and we have guarded your secret well; so well that not
even one of our gossiping neighbors knows but you are
our own flesh and blood.

Mercy. [*Covering her face with her hands.*] Papa, can
it be that I am a foundling? If so, merciful Heaven protect me.

Deacon. No, you are nothing of the kind; you are our
own dear child still. There, don't take on so, or I shall
think Maggie was right. See, here are a few trinkets, a
bit of a chain and bracelet, which were in the basket.
[*Clasps it around her wrist.*] There, see how nicely it fits.
You must always keep them, child; for I suppose they
were your mother's.

Mercy. Why, why did I not know of this before?

Deacon. For my part I shall be sorry you know it
now if you don't stop grieving over it. Come, cheer up,
and read your letter while I run up to the mill. I'll be
back in a few minutes, and go home with you if you'll wait.

Mercy. Yes, papa, I want to think.   [*Exit Deacon.*

Jack. [*To Ledyard.*] A capital time to secure her while
the old fellow's gone.

Ledyard. Yes, but we must wait till he's out of hearing.
I hope Tim is ready by the border of the forest with the
close carriage.

Jack. Never fear for Tim; he's all right.

Mercy. [*Opens her letter and reads.*

"DEAREST MERCY: Next week is set for my first appearance in opera, and Baratoli tells me I shall succeed.
Madam Elva, the present prima donna, has become terribly jealous of me. At times she frightens me half out of
my wits by her savage looks. But I came near forgetting
the most important part of my epistle. I have again seen
the stranger of the wood, he who first mentioned the
name of Baratoli to me. His name is Oscar Alma. I
first saw him at the opera in company with Pauline,
Baratoli's niece, whom the Madam tells me he is going to
marry and take abroad with him. We passed very near
him, but he did not see me. Oh, how I longed to fall on
my knees to him and thank him for his kindly advice to

me; but I met the basilisk gaze of Pauline and drew back. Oh that I could make him understand the true character of the woman he is about to wed! But what would he think of my interference—I, a beggar, a slave until he pronounced the name of Baratoli? He will marry her, and I am powerless to prevent."

Mercy. [*Clasping her hands and dropping the letter.*] Oh Bessie, darling Bessie! your words are as a dagger to my heart! He, my adored Alma, ere now the husband of another? and I but yesterday received a letter from him conched in the glowing language of love! Oh, the perfidy of man! [*Draws the letter of Alma from her bosom and tears it in pieces.*] So perish my love for thee, unworthy Alma!

Ledyard to Jack. So the artist is playing a double game; ha! ha! She's a bird worth the catching, though.

Jack. Yes, and we'd best be about it, or the deacon'll be back!

Ledyard. [*Springing out.*] Come on, then!

[*Mercy beholds them and attempts to fly, but is caught by Jack. Screams. Enter Deacon Wilde, rushes on Jack, Ledyard fires on him, he falls, and Ledyard and Jack escape with Mercy.*

SCENE II.—*Room in Deacon Wilde's cottage.*

Enter WILL LITTLEFIELD, MARK KENDRICK, *several villagers.* MRS. WILDE *knitting.*

Will. Good evening, Mistress Wilde. Thought we'd stop and have a little bit of a frolic, being we were passing; but where's Mercy?

Mrs. W. She took her book and went off to the glen a long time ago. Justice got a letter out of the post-office for her, so he said he would go through the glen on his way to the mill and bring her back with him.

Mark. It's a poor place—that glen—for a girl like Mercy to spend so much time in!

Mrs. W. That's just what I tell Justice. I get worried enamost tu death 'bout her, she stays out there so late; it's so lonesome that it makes my flesh creep every time I go through it by daylight.

Enter DEACON WILDE, *with blood on his clothes.*

Mrs. W. Sakes alive! deacon, where have you been, and what's become of Mercy?

Deacon. She's gone! They've carried her off. [*Wrings his hands.*] Oh! what shall I do, what shall I do?

Will. Gone where? Pray explain at once.

Mark. Speak, for heaven's sake, and let us go in quest of her! Who are they?

Mrs. W. Justice, Justice, who has got her?

Deacon. I don't know! I can't tell! two rough-looking men; they shot me in the arm [*women scream*] and then dragged her away.

Mrs. W. Oh, this is dreadful! Won't some one go for the neighbors?

Enter RACHEL SNOW.

Will. Mark, you run over to the squire's; get firearms and all the help you can, and I will go to Dikeman's and the parson's. We must scour the forest without delay.
[*Exit boys.*

Rachel. What 'pon airth do you stand there wringing your hands for, Miss Wilde? You don't expect that's a going to bring your darter back, do you? You'd better be a binding up your husband's arm.

Deacon. Don't trouble yourself about my arm, Rachel; it's only a flesh wound; but try and do something comforting for Maggie. Just make her a cup of tea and toast while I go out again to search for my child. [*Exit.*

Rachel. Well, if this aren't the curiousest mess I ever got into in my born days! There's been foul play somewhere! I allers thought the Wildes would get into trouble marrying as they did; and now they can see what they've got by it.

Maggie. Oh, my child! my blessed child!

Rachel. Just to hear that critter take on though. It beats all nature, it does. Well, when folks makes idols of their children they must expect to have them taken away; that's all the consolation I can give! As for tea and toast, I reckon Mistress Maggie aren't so far gone but she can make it herself.

2*

SCENE III.—*Cave of the Knights of the Red Crescent.—Lethridge sits before a table; torches, bottles, and glasses.*

Enter MAXWELL.

Lethridge. You are doubtless surprised at the hasty summons, Maxwell, but we have to initiate a new knight into our order. Denville Lowbury has come hither to join us.

Max. Ha, ha! let's drink to his success. [*Both drink.*

Lethridge. Wetherbe should have been here ere this. By what accident is he detained?

Max. I have noticed a change in him since we buried his Annie.

Lethridge. Pshaw! that will soon blow over; he was not wont to loiter; but let us proceed to business. [*Whistles, and Lowbury enters.*] Young man, we Knights of the Red Crescent believe in the laws of equality; that is to say, you have the same right in Parson Beverly's pulpit that he has, provided you have the strength of arm to enforce the claim. You have an equal right with John Dikeman to the chickens on his roost, provided you secure them, and don't get caught in the trap. You have a right to the sleek horses driven by the squire, provided you can trot them over the line into Canada. You have the best right to the deacon's pretty daughter, provided you can catch her. The cage is ready for the bird, and a pretty dove-cote it is, too; so you had best set about laying the snare.

Lowbury. But if we are detected?

Lethridge. The Knights of the Red Crescent are never detected; and, remember, we have no " ifs " in our vocabulary. Maxwell, bring the book. [*Maxwell brings book and stand.*] Place your hand on that book, Lowbury, and repeat after me the creed. [*Lowbury lays his hand on the Bible and repeats.*] Before these witnesses, and with my hand on the sacred book, do I, Denville Lowbury, swear allegiance to the captain of this most noble order. Hereafter, so long as we both may live, I faithfully promise to fulfil his commands, to obey to the letter his slightest wishes, to break all other ties, and live only to the good of this divine order.

Lethridge. In token whereof I decorate you with this

symbol. [*Places on Lowbury the scarf and crescent of the order.*] And now, in the presence of these witnesses, I pronounce you a Knight of the Red Crescent.

Enter WETHERBE. *Throws down a turkey.*

Wetherbe. Hilloa, cap., what's up?
Lethridge. A new knight to our glorious order.
                    [*Wetherbe and Lowbury shake hands.*
Maxwell. Now for a bumper and a song!
                    [*Fills glasses. Lethridge sings.*

SONG.

Here's health to the knights of the jolly Red Crescent!
Free and easy's their style, and their life it is pleasant;
They ride the best steeds of the country around,
And the choicest of game in their larder is found.

CHORUS.   [*All join.*
            Then ho, for the knights of the red!
        Ho! ho, for the knights of the red!
                There's a wink and a smile
                The fair lass to beguile;
            Ho! ho for the knights of the red!

No captain e'er marshalled so fearless a crew,
Hurra for the Red Knights! avaunt with your blue!
To one color we rally, our knights never fly;
Red Crescents we've lived, jolly reds we will die!

CHORUS.
            Then hurra! for the knights of the red!
        Hip, hurra! for the knights of the red!
                There's a wink and a smile
                The fair lass to beguile;
            Hip, hurra! for the knights of the red!
                            [*All drink.*

Lethridge. Pray explain your absence; our knights are not wont to tarry after a summons.
Wetherbe. There's a terrible stir abroad, captain; men, women, and children all in the streets with lanterns, pick-axes, and old rusty guns that haven't been loaded since the Revolution. I kept shady at first, for fear they were on my scent; for you know it was but yesterday I helped

to run off the squire's mare over the border; but I soon found it was sweet Mercy, the deacon's daughter, who was missing,—kidnapped, as the story goes.

Lowbury. [*Springing up.*] What! How?

Lethridge. Keep cool, boy. Go on, Wetherbe.

Wetherbe. I've but little more to tell. Meeting Rachel, the gossip, I made inquiries, and learned that Mercy was walking alone in the glen, when two ill-looking fellows seized her and were bearing her away; but her screams brought her father to her rescue. He was fired upon by the rowdies and left wounded on the field, while they escaped with their booty. Rachel says, when he arrived at his own door, he looked as if he had committed murder himself.

Lethridge. A thought strikes me! I'll have the old deacon arraigned for murder, provided the girl don't turn up to prevent it. Won't I pay off the old coon now, though!

Lowbury. I do not believe the tale. Rachel is too much of a gossip to tell the truth, you know.

Wetherbe. Yes, I know; but the girl is gone, fast enough. I remained until every nook and corner of the forest was searched. Rachel says, if it was not that the deacon is a church-member, she should think he had put her out of the way himself, to keep her from marrying you, Lowbury!

Lethridge. Rachel will be an important witness in the case!

Lowbury. Depend upon it, that is one of Rachel's lies.

Lethridge. Never mind that! all the better for me if he is arrested! I believe, Wetherbe, the lost girl somewhat resembled your Annie.

Wetherbe. Only in the size and color of the hair.

Lethridge. Sufficient for my purpose, however!

Wetherbe. What the devil are you up to now, Lethridge?

Lethridge. The deacon shall be arrested to-morrow morning, before sunrise, for the murder of his daughter. This night the body of your lost Annie must be exhumed and thrown into the creek near where Mercy Wilde was last seen. I will see that it is brought out of the creek in the proper time to fasten suspicion on the old man as her murderer. In your care, Wetherbe, I leave this business; see that it is done before dawn!

Wetherbe. Good heavens, captain! this is too much.

Lethridge. Remember! there is nothing impossible with the Knights of the Red Crescent! Maxwell will accompany you. You, Denville Lowbury, had better remain here for a week or so; it may help on the suspicion. You will find eatables in the vault below. If you are fond of reading, here are "Tom Paine's Works" and "Daring Deeds of Highwaymen," both interesting in their way.

Lowbury. But Mercy; should she return——

Lethridge. She is yours, by the honor of the captain of the Red Crescent.   [*Join hands.*

Lowbury. Perhaps I ought to tell you that I met Mercy in the glen last night.

Lethridge. And she refused you?

Lowbury. She did, sir; in despair I sought the cave, resolved to join your order.

Lethridge. You did nobly! If the girl is living it shall bring her to your arms!

Lowbury. [*Aside.*] I never felt myself so firmly in the devil's grasp as now.

SCENE IV.—*Liverpool.—Room in Hotel.—Mercy Wilde sitting by table.*

Enter LEDYARD THORRINGTON, MERCY *rising as he enters.*

Mercy. What means this continued imprisonment, sir? Did you not tell me I should have my liberty immediately on my arrival?

Ledyard. Ha! ha! Your simplicity is charming, my sweet one!

Mercy. Is it not enough to tear me from home and parents, to brand me as a maniac the better to carry out your vile scheme——

Ledyard. [*Attempting to put his arms around her.*] Hold, my pretty coz! I'll assure you I'm doing what is for your future good; you will soon thank me——

Mercy. Never, never sir! Leave me, I command you! Your presence here inspires me with contempt!

Ledyard. What will you say, little one, when I tell you, you are not the offspring of the simple-hearted Wildes?

Mercy. [*Aside.*] Can it be possible that he knows aught of my parentage? [*To Thorrington.*] What authority have you for saying that, sir?

Ledyard. The best evidence, my sweet Mercy, that the world can produce. You are my cousin, and as such I am willing to take you under my own protection, to raise you from the humble sphere in which you have so long lived to that in which I move; in fact, I have resolved to make you my wife!

Mercy. An honorable way of declaring your intentions, sir. I beg you to understand, once for all, that I will submit to a dungeon for life rather than become the wife of a villain!

Ledyard. When next we meet you will be in a better mood for wooing, miss!   [*Turns to leave.*

Mercy. Hold, sir! You have said I was not the daughter of Justice and Margaret Wilde. Before you leave I desire you to explain yourself.

Ledyard. The pretty dear queens it well! when in a better temper she shall know more! [*Exit, locking the door. Mercy rushes forward and attempts to open it, but in vain; sinks on her knees.*] Just Heaven! remember thy daughter in her sorrows; and in mercy send thou a messenger to my relief! [*Rises, sees a key before her; picks it up.*] What! a skeleton key! if it would release me! [*Tries it in the door, opens it, hears steps, closes it and puts on a shawl and bonnet, listens, peeps out.*] I will make the attempt; and now, Heaven guide me!   [*Exit Mercy.*

SCENE V.—*The Green-room of the Opera.—Bessie makes her debut as Prima Donna.*

Enter ELVA *and* PAULINE.

Pauline. After all your threats, the girl still lives; ay, and bids fair to become the rage.

Elva. Her days are numbered!

Pauline. You said the same at the rehearsal three weeks ago, and she not only lives, but thrives under the teachings of my silly uncle. Ha! ha! to think of an old head like yours being set aside by a silly young wench. How did you relish the reception, my lady, and her encores? Why, Elva, the boards are fairly ringing yet; don't you hear? [*Elva walks back and forth with a distressed air. Bessie's voice is heard singing; applause, etc.*] There, Elva, there! don't you enjoy it? It is her closing act. What a round of applause!

[*Elva tears her hair with rage.*

Elva. [*Taking a bottle and glass from a cupboard.*] She will be exhausted with her efforts. I will see that she gets a dose this time.

Pauline. There, it is over; I hear them coming. As I do not desire to be a witness, I will retire, wishing you success, however. You know the old adage, Elva : "The devil pipes luck to his own." [*Exit Pauline.*

Enter the MADAM, *leading* BESSIE, BARATOLI *and critics following.*

Madam B. Oh, Elva! it was such a triumph! What a pity that your part took you off the stage just as she came in with the last solo. Oh, it was magnificent, it was heavenly!

Elva. [*Aside.*] I a witness to her triumphs? Never, never, never! All shall be witness to another tragedy, in which she plays the first part.

To Bessie. You are quite gone, I see. I know what a first appearance is. Why, you are about to faint! Here, take some wine; Pauline brought it for you.

[*Hands a glass to Bessie, who takes a swallow.*

Bessie. But look at the seignior; he, too, is overworked; excuse my having tasted. [*Hands him the glass.*] Do me the honor.

Seignior B. Your lips, dear child, have sweetened it. [*Drinks.*] Ah! it is refreshing indeed.

Elva. [*Springing forward.*] Hold! Baratoli, for the love of heaven, till I get——

Seignior B. Why do you look so agitated, Elva?

Madam B. [*Aside.*] A little jealous; don't you see? The triumph of our protégée affects her seriously.

[*Madam Elva throws the bottle of wine on the floor.*

Elva. [*Aside.*]   The devil's work is done.

[*Exit Elva.*
[*Baratoli staggers, turns pale, falls.*
Madam. My son, are you ill?   Help! help!
Bessie. The good seignior!   Oh! my head.
[*Bessie is near falling ; is caught, and supported by
   one of the critics ; the Madam kneels by her son,
   chafes his temples ; all is confusion.*
Madam. Oh, my son! my son! art thou dying?
Run for a physician !

SCENE VI.—*Liverpool.*—*Drawing-room in the private
residence of Mr. and Mrs. John Stilwell.*—*Mercy
asleep on the sofa, bonnet partially off, leaving her fea-
tures visible.*

Enter JOHN STILWELL *and his wife.*

Eliza. [*Looking at Mercy.*]   I don't believe a word
you say, John, about this young woman.   She has too
pretty a face to be tramping about the country in this
style.
John. Very well, Eliza, turn her out of doors if you
like ; only don't let the sin lay at my door if she starves
in the street.   But I must be off to meet Ayelton.   You
see I shall have to bring him by force if we get him here
at all.
Eliza. True, and it's time the company were assem-
bling now.   I say, John, are you sure that sleeping beauty
isn't one of your London flames come down on the sly ?
John. Eliza, for shame ! to suspect me of fanning a
London flame ! especially here in Liverpool.
Eliza. John, look me in the eye !   [*John looks steadily
for a moment.*]   Well, I shall have to believe you
whether I will or no !
John. [*Kissing her.*]   Good-by, love !   Don't forget
to dispose of your beauty there before the guests arrive,
or it might make it awkward.
Eliza. [*Clapping her hands.*]   A lucky thought strikes
me, John.   [*Gives him a heavy slap on the cheek.*
John. [*Rubbing his cheek.*]   Pray let the thought in-
stead of yourself strike me next time !
Eliza. Won't she make a beautiful Morning to my

Night? I declare those golden curls look just like sunrise! *[Springs to Mercy's side and shakes her.*

John. I'm exit before the explosion.   *[Exit John.*

Eliza. Wake up, my dear; wake up!

Mercy. [*Looking wildly around.*] Where am I? Oh, I have been dreaming. I thought I was in my dear, quiet home, and my mother had come to waken me.

[Weeps.

Eliza. There, there, dear child! don't cry and spoil those fine eyes. My husband has told me your sad story, and I'm very sorry for you; so sorry that I'm going to make you very happy while you stay with us!

Mercy. But if I could only go back to my friends in America.

Eliza. And so you shall, in the next steamer that sails, which is in two weeks. My husband has a friend who is down from London to take passage, and he will put you under his care. In the meantime I expect you to be my guest, and as such you must appear at my fancy-dress ball to-night.

Mercy. If you will please excuse me——

Eliza. Not I, indeed! I appear as Night; you are just the one to take the opposite character of Aurora or Morning; so come with me to my dressing-room at once. Come! we have no time to tarry.

[Pulls Mercy out. Exit both.

Enter Mr. JOHN STILWELL *and* Sir WILLIAM AYELTON.

Sir Wm. Though you may not be willing to confess it, you have made a great mistake in bringing me here, Stilwell.

John. I trust not, Sir William! Shake off your accustomed melancholy for once, and appear like a sane man.

Sir Wm. Impossible! my dear sir. The memory of my lost Constance has become, as it were, a part of my existence; and lately I have seen a portrait which promises to afford me a clew to her last resting-place.

John. Ay, and that accounts for your sudden journey to America.

Sir Wm. Yes, I have the assurance that she died

there, and I have another hope so visionary that I scarcely dare name it—that of finding a daughter.

John. And I have a lady here, a true-born American, who takes passage in the next steamer for New York. Nay, don't scowl, Sir William, she is beautiful as the houris, and will make a most entertaining companion.

Sir Wm. Don't ask it of me, Stilwell; you know my aversion to the companionship of even a handsome lady.

Enter ELIZA, *followed by* MERCY, *in costume.*

John. Here she comes. There is no help for you, Sir William, so bear it like a man. [*Leads Eliza up.*] This dark-eyed beauty, in her starlit mantle, is Night, and this is Aurora, or Morning, alias the pretty American.

Sir Wm. My Constance! [*Embraces her. Mercy is frightened; screams.*

John. What the devil are you doing? I expected you to admire, not devour her! [*Releases Mercy.*

Sir Wm. It is she! my child! the daughter of my lost Constance!

Eliza. But she tells us she left parents in America— plain farmers, were they not?

Mercy. They were my foster-parents. I had supposed them my real parents until the night I was so cruelly torn from their arms; then my father disclosed the secret, that I was left when an infant at his door.

Sir Wm. And was there no letter, no word to tell them of your parentage and name?

Mercy. No, sir; nothing but my clothing and this bracelet and necklace.

Sir Wm. [*Examining bracelet.*] Heaven be praised! That bracelet I gave my Constance on her wedding-day. Inside, in small Roman characters, you'll find the name of Constance Ayelton. [*John takes and examines it.*

John. True, true! I congratulate you, Sir William. Pray what do you think of my mistake in bringing you here?

Sir Wm. I can never sufficiently thank you.

Eliza. And now you will not have to make that dread voyage.

Mercy. My dear foster-parents are suffering untold agony at my absence.

Sir Wm. And there is a lone grave there that we must search out—the grave of my lost Constance. We will go, as was first intended, love; for I see by your eyes you wish it.

Enter Guests in dominoes and fancy costumes.

Eliza. Do not withdraw from the company, Sir William. I'm sure if you ever felt like dancing, it ought to be to-night. [*Guests make their respects to John and Eliza. Sets form for quadrille ; dance.*

SCENE VII.—*A room in Baratoli's house.—Bessie ill on a couch.*

Enter ELVA *stealthily.*

Bessie. Oh, I have been ill so long. That terrible night —when Elva seemed so like a demon and gave me the sickening wine——

Elva. [*Aside.*] Sickening wine! ha! ha! Curses, curses on her! [*To Bessie.*] Look, you wretch, beggar; you who have dared to cross my path ; you who thought to supplant me in the love of Baratoli; it was you who put the poison to his lips : ha! ha! take this consoling thought with you. Had you drunk the wine yourself you might have saved him. You killed him, not I !

Bessie. Oh, cruel-hearted woman! Would to heaven I had. I would die a thousand deaths to save my Baratoli one pang ; but too late, too late ! Would that I could die too !

Elva. Dying would be too great a blessing for such as you. Live on, and suffer, ha! ha!   [*Exit Elva.*

Enter PAULINE. BESSIE *rises.*

Bessie. My good Pauline, will you not let me look upon the good Seignior's face once more? Now that he is dead there can be no harm ; then I will go away and never trouble you again.

Pauline. You will, ha! You're getting really clever ; but if I mistake not you'll go without even a look at the seignior ! I'm mistress here now, so start yourself ! [*Throws her a purse.*] There, take that and never let me see your face again. [*Bessie puts on a bonnet and shawl and walks slowly towards the door. To Pauline.*

Bessie. Will you tell the good madam that I left her my blessing and many thanks for all her kindness to me?

Pauline. No! I'll tell her nothing; leave at once, or I'll call the police!

Bessie. [*Clasping her hands.*] Alas! where shall I go? Home and friends I have none.   [*Exit Bessie.*

ACT IV.

SCENE I.—*Deacon Wilde's house in Alderly.—Sitting-Room.—Rachel Snow bustling about.*

Rachel. Justice Wilde might have got a better house-keeper than Maggie Wrinkle, and not looked far either; but some folks never know when they're well off. As I said to Mr. Beverly, says I, there's Bessie Dikeman come home worse off than when she went away, I reckon, if the truth is known. She goes moping around with fine ladyish airs; but that don't affect me in the least. I always knew she had no voice for singing, and I reckon that big Bear-toller got sick enough of her, or he wouldn't have sent her home. [*A rap is heard.*] Lordy massa! Come in.   [*Smooths her hair, adjusts her apron.*

Enter WILL LITTLEFIELD.

Rachel. Lawful sakes! Will, is that you? I'm dreadful glad to see you; but what's the matter?

Will. [*Throwing himself into a chair.*] Matter enough. There was a body fished up out of the creek last night! I know it wasn't the body of Mercy Wilde; but the jury have convicted the deacon of the murder, and he's got to be hung—bo! ho! ho!

Rachel. Well, don't take on so, William, dear! there's women left yet in the world to comfort ye! [*Rachel attempts to embrace him. Exit Will.*] Bo! ho! ho!

Rachel. Was there ever such a born fool as that William? I wouldn't marry him if he was to get down on

his knees to me; that I wouldn't. [*Rap at door.*] Lawful
sakes! company again? Come in, I say!

Enter ALMA *and* MR. THOMAS THORRINGTON.

Goodness, Mr. Alma, I didn't expect to see you back
so soon, but take a chair, du. [*Pushes a chair towards
him.*] And this old fellow maybe'd like to set down tu.
[*Gives him a chair.*

Alma. I expected to have been here sooner though,
Miss Rachel; but how are all the good folks, and whither
fled?

Rachel. Maybe you haven't heard the news. I thought
at first you'd come up to the hanging.

Alma. Hanging! for Heaven's sake explain yourself.

Rachel. Why, the deacon's daughter, Mercy—you
know her—took a master sight of pains painting her picture too,—well, she turned up missing a few months ago,
and her father was arrested and tried for her murder.

Alma. But she is not dead, my darling Mercy! No,
no! I'll not believe it!

Rachel. Hold on, sir, till I finish the story! Her
body was fished up out of the creek yesterday, and on
that evidence they have convicted the deacon, and he's
going to be hung next week.

Thomas T. Alas, alas! Heaven has already put it
out of my power to render reparation to my Constance's
child, if this horrid tale be true.

Alma. [*Terribly excited.*] Tell me, pray tell me where
is Mrs. Wilde, that I may sympathize with her in this
bereavement.

Rachel. She is in the bedroom, sir; won't see anybody
except the parson and Bessie Dikeman, as if she thought
they could help her.

Alma. Pray tell her I am here, and must speak with
her on business at once!

Rachel. I'll tell her; but 't won't do no good.

[*Exit Rachel.*

Thomas T. What can this mean, sir? I thought those
people, her parents, were Christians, not butchers!

Alma. And so they are, sir. There is some terrible oversight here, believe me! If they persist in hanging Deacon Wilde they will hang an innocent man!

Thomas T. I have heard much of the laxity of the laws of the United States. Is this an example, Mr. Alma?

Alma. Wait, my dear sir, till we get at the facts of the case. Rachel is an inveterate gossip, and we must not believe all she says.

Enter MRS. WILDE, *leaning on the arm of* BROWN BESSIE. *Embraces* ALMA, *and weeps upon his neck.*

Alma. Calm yourself, my dear madam, and tell me if this horrible tale is true.

Mrs. W. That Mercy, our darling, is gone, is too true; but I do not, cannot believe her dead; nor is my husband a murderer. Before Heaven will I take my oath of that.

Alma. But the body that was found—did you see it?

Mrs. W. Yes, both Bessie and I, and I could have sworn it was not hers; but our evidence was not allowed. You see they are fierce as hounds for his blood, and nothing but hanging will satisfy them. [*Weeps.*

Alma. [*To Bessie.*] And who is this? My little brown maid of the wood, as I live!

Bessie. Yes, sir, the same; and I have so longed to behold you again, to thank you for the mention of the name of that noble man.

Alma. Then you did go to Baratoli?

Bessie. I did: and the only happy moments of my life were those spent under his instruction, in his hospitable mansion; but it is past; and the only happiness left me is that of rendering sweet incense to his memory in the songs he loved.

Alma. What mean you? Hath any harm happened to my friend?

Bessie. I was driven from his mansion, when he was dying, by his niece, Pauline. I could have forgiven all had I been permitted to have seen his face once more,

and bade farewell to his mother; but both were denied
me; and being myself ill, I had no alternative but to return to my humble home. On arriving I found others
in deep sorrow as well as myself. Dear Mercy was gone,
and her parents distracted; and now the worst of all is
the terrible fate that awaits the poor innocent old man,
her father!

> [*Alma covers his face with his hands. Thomas ap-*
> *proaches Mrs. Wilde.*

Thomas T. My dear madam, I too have had trials
and afflictions, but perhaps not as severe as your own. I
had one child, a daughter; we called her Constance; but
she had the same sweet expression of face as your daughter Mercy. She married in opposition to my wishes, and
I separated her from her husband, bringing her to America. I think it must have been in this vicinity that I
left her and returned to New York. In my absence she
died, and her infant—a little girl—I supposed died with
her. I have since been led to believe the child living.
Can you give me no information regarding a motherless
child?

Mrs. W. Hold, sir! Why do you come at this late
hour to seek that which was lost seventeen years ago?

Thomas. To make restitution to that child; to crave
forgiveness of her for the wrongs done her mother.

Mrs. W. Mercy was not our child. She was left, a
foundling, on our steps, when an infant, but no one suspected it.

Thomas. Was there nothing left by which to identify
her?

Mrs. W. A plenty of infant's clothing, and a chain
and bracelet. The bracelet had a curious mark on it;
Justice said it was some foreign language, he reckoned,
but we could neither of us read it. She had both the
chain and bracelet on when she was lost.

Thomas. I have no doubt but the lost Mercy is my
granddaughter. Oh, that I had arrived in time to save
her!

Alma. Would that I had never left her. [*Draws a*
golden curl from his bosom.] Behold this treasured curl!
her parting gift. Worlds could not buy it from me now.

> [*All weep.*

SCENE II.—*Court-yard in front of the jail.—Scaffold with rope.—Lethridge, Maxwell, Mark, Kendrick, Will Littlefield, and villagers present.*

DENVILLE LOWBURY *and* RAB WETHERBE *enter, also* THOMAS THORRINGTON *and* ALMA.

Lethridge. [*To Max.*] Wasn't the artist and the parson warmble-croped, tho', when they found that their evidence wouldn't be admitted?

Max. It does beat the devil, though, where that gal is. She may turn up yet!

Lethridge. She'll have to be on hand in less than five minutes if she expects to save the deacon's neck! [*Deacon enters slowly, followed by the sheriff.*] There he comes up to time. I'll tell you, Max, he's an old brick, the deacon is. [*Steps upon the scaffold.*

Will Littlefield. [*To Alma.*] O Lordy massa! it's awful, it is! I du say, Mr. Alma, to hang an innocent man in this way!

Alma. I've sent a man with a petition to the governor for pardon. I hope he may arrive in time.

[*Lowbury disappears.*

Lethridge. He's going to die game, he is; ha! ha! a speech!

Max. Do keep still, Lethridge, let's hear what he says.

Deacon Wilde. Although not guilty of the great and terrible crime charged upon me, and for which I am about to suffer, still, let not any misconstrue my reiterations of innocence into a desire to escape the punishment fixed by law upon me. I find no fault with the charge of the Judge or the verdict of the jury. They, doubtless, feel that in their decision they have obeyed the dictates of conscience in acceding to the demands of justice.

I am not unhappy at the prospect of leaving this for a brighter, and more enduring home. If those who have part or lot in my arrest and trial have a clear conscience, then the mere matter of pushing me into heaven a few months, weeks, or days sooner than I should otherwise go, will surely be no injustice to me; and if in after years my innocence should be established, let not those who have been the unwilling instruments of my death render themselves unhappy. If there is an offence, may Heaven forgive them, as I do now! Sheriff, I am ready.

[*Sheriff adjusts the cap and rope, raises the ax: a cry among the crowd.*

Enter DEN. LOWBURY, *with* MERCY *and* SIR WM. AYELTON.

Denville. Hold, hold! [*Mercy springs upon the scaffold and clasps Deacon Wilde in her arms.*

Mercy. My papa, my dear papa! To think you were so near death and I knew nothing of your danger!

Deacon Wilde. My child, my child!

Lethridge. What a devilish blunder! Come, Maxwell, I reckon we may as well make ourselves scarce.

Denville. [*Grasping Lethridge by the collar.*] No, you don't, sir! Come on, boys! help me to hold him! This is the rascal that had the deacon arrested, though he knew he was innocent! He it was who caused the dead body of Annie Melbourn to be thrown into the creek, and then swore to its being that of Mercy Wilde, for the sake of getting the deacon hung!

Will Littlefield. Come on! shall the gallows be cheated of its victim? I say come on!

[*Crowd rush on Lethridge, and attempt to put him on the scaffold.*

Deacon Wilde. My friends, do not hurry a poor sinful creature into eternity. If guilty, as you say, let the proper authorities arrest and give him a lawful trial, and may Heaven have mercy on him. [*Lethridge is led away by sheriff. Mercy walks along with Deacon Wilde.*

Alma. Mercy, my darling, have you no word for me in all your joy? [*Looks coldly on him.*

Mercy. I hope and trust you are happy, sir. [*To her father.*] Dear papa, this is the dear, kind parent who has been more than a father to me; if you love him but half as much as I it will be sufficient. [*Deacon Wilde and Sir William shake hands cordially.*

Will Littlefield. Bo! ho! ho! I never was so tickled in all my life! I wonder what I'm crying for.

Alma. [*Aside.*] Alas, that cold, indifferent look; that cruel stare! Have her altered fortunes so changed her already? Then farewell to all my hopes of happiness.

3

SCENE III.—*Drawing-room in the Cottage of Deacon Wilde.—Mercy walking back and forth, apparently in deep thought.*

Enter BESSIE, *robed in black.*

Bessie. Dearest Mercy, have we met again?

> [*Embrace.*

Mercy. Again! It seems years, my beloved Bessie, since we parted! Oh, my brain is still giddy with the terrible scenes of the past few days.

Bessie. And I, oh, Mercy! I can never, never tell you what I have suffered. I, who was only a few weeks ago so happy; but he is dead, the generous, the noble Baratoli, and I again a houseless wanderer.

Mercy. Say not so, dearest Bessie. Your home shall be in future with me. My noble father will love you for my sake. But tell me of your friends; are they happy—the artist and Pauline—whom you wrote me were to be married?

Bessie. The Madam was misinformed; it seems Mr. Alma never intended to marry Pauline, though it was she who spread the report that they were engaged. I have met him here, and I fancy he looks unhappy : but, dear Mercy, you are ill.

Mercy. Excuse me, a little faint, that is all. Don't mention it to papa; he is so fearful he shall lose me again that he scarce allows me out of his sight; but here he comes with strangers—a distinguished looking man. [*Bessie looks, screams, and rushes into the arms of Madam Baratoli. The Seignior takes her from his mother's arms.*

Seignior. Bless my heart, sweet Bessie; as pale as a lily; but what possessed you to run away from us in all our troubles?

Bessie. I run away, sir! Oh! Pauline nearly broke my heart by telling me that you were dead, and that the good Madam refused to see me. She bade me leave the house, and thinking I had lost all my friends, what could I do but obey? Oh! it seems a horrid dream to me.

Madam. The wicked wretch. She told us you had

been decoyed off by some opera troupe that travelled about the country.

Baratoli. Neither Elva's devilish plots nor Pauline's malice shall part us again; never, never, Bessie. [*Winds his arm about her, and Bessie lays her hand in his.*

Madam. You must be married at once; come, Bessie, do you hear? I have bought bridal robes, and a crown of diamonds, such as befits the bride of Baratoli.

Baratoli. Yes, my beloved. I am impatient to call you my own. [*Exit Sir William Baratoli, Madam, Bessie.*

Enter ALMA, *with his prize picture of* MERCY.

Alma. Pardon my venturing into your presence again, once-loved Mercy.

Mercy. [*Aside.*] Once loved!

Alma. In my disinterested affection I forgot that to you title and wealth had arisen, forming an inseparable barrier between us. The treasured portrait I return, feeling that I have no longer a right to keep it.

Mercy. Oh, Oscar, if you loved me still; but no, no; you desire to be released; I thought,– I heard you were the husband of another, and that is why––why I——

Alma. [*Clasping her in his arms.*] And you love me still?

Enter SIR WILLIAM AYELTON.

Mercy. With my whole heart.

Sir William. So ho! so ho! What is all this?

Mercy. Dearest father, has not papa Wilde told you I was engaged to Mr. Alma before he left America for London?

Sir William. Not a lisp have I heard till now; I had my suspicions, however; but the very cool reception you gave Mr. Alma on your first meeting quite lulled them.

Mercy. A little misunderstanding, father, that is all.

Sir William. [*To Alma.*] I can never lose my daughter, sir; you understand?

Mercy. Perhaps you prefer gaining a son, dear papa.

Sir William. I do, my child, and you must make Mr. Alma understand that, and sign the agreement.

Alma. Anything, everything, so I only secure the fair one!

Sir William. And now, dear Mercy, I present you with the jewels designed for your mother years ago.

[*Presents her with a casket.*

Alma. And I am entrusted with a casket from your grandfather, Thomas Thorrington. It contains the jewels that were your mother's before marriage: he begs you will accept them as a gift from her. [*To Sir William.*] Is it too much, Sir William, to ask you to forgive and grant the old man an interview?

[*His brow darkens and he paces the floor.*

Mercy. [*Aside to Alma.*] Bring him in. I cannot be happy till they are reconciled.   [*Exit Alma.*

Sir William. [*Taking jewels from the box, presented by Thomas.*] Put them on, dear child! there; I could fancy it was herself before me, you are so very like her.

[*Enter Thomas, followed by Alma.*

Thomas. [*To Sir William.*] Can you not find it in your heart to forgive one who has suffered nearly as much as yourself?

Mercy. Dear father, let me be the link that binds your two hearts together.   [*Takes a hand of each.*

Enter BARATOLI, *leading* BESSIE; *the* MADAM, MR. *and* MRS. WILDE, WILL LITTLEFIELD, RACHEL SNOW, *and principal characters.* MERCY *leaves her father and grandfather, and joins hands with* ALMA, *who stands beside* BESSIE *and* BARATOLI *in centre of the stage.*

Will. [*Aside.*] Well, I guess I sha'n't get her after all. That confounded picture-painter is ahead of my time?

Rachel. [*Aside.*] I allers said I'd never marry young.

www.ingramcontent.com/pod-product-compliance
Lightning Source LLC
Chambersburg PA
CBHW030902260626
47169CB00008B/2646